ELLIE DOESN'T UNDERSTAND CHILDREN. She doesn't understand what they want or what makes them happy. She doesn't understand why they're so mean.

Adults are no better. Her mother spends her days consoling sad, lonely men, mysteriously easing their grief; men like Funeral Lou, lost in his own sorrow, tenderly embalming the dead.

Only Joseph offers Ellie a ray of hope, pointing to a brighter path through the darkness, his carved tiger a symbol of beauty in a morally ambiguous world. A world full of conflicted souls like Gregory, the man Ellie meets in the park, with the colourful, unusual fruit...

STRANGE FRUIT

A haunting tale of a young girl's coming-of-age; a dazzling narrative of heartache and hope.

Strange Fruit

STRANGE FRUIT

James Cooper

2014

STRANGE FRUIT
Copyright © James Cooper 2014

COVER ART
Copyright © Tomislav Tikulin 2014

Published in March 2014 by PS Publishing Ltd. by arrangement with the author. All rights reserved by the author.

The right of James Cooper to be identified as the Author of this Work has been asserted by him in accordance with the Copyright, Designs and Patents Act 1988.

First Edition

ISBN
978-1-848637-23-8
978-1-848637-24-5 (signed edition)

This book is a work of Fiction. Names, characters, places and incidents either are products of the author's imagination or are used fictitiously. Any resemblance to actual events or locales or persons, living or dead, is entirely coincidental.

Design & Layout by Michael Smith

Printed and bound in England by T.J. International

PS Publishing Ltd
Grosvenor House
1 New Road, Hornsea
HU18 1PG, England

editor@pspublishing.co.uk
www.pspublishing.co.uk

For Ethan

STRANGE FRUIT

SOMETIMES, LATE AT NIGHT, WHEN I'M TUCKED UP IN bed, I can hear men screaming in the house. They are crying; burying their head in my mother's lap and weeping for the loved ones they've lost. They come to my mother for help. Sad, lonely men, many of them dishevelled with haunted faces, like the old ladies I see walking to the shops in the rain. They are desperate, my mother tells me; in need of comfort and support. They are happy to pay good money to hear the reassuring words they know my mother can provide. She tells me that, one day, *I* might lose someone I love, and I fall silent. What she means is I might lose *her*. She is trying to make me feel sorry for something I've done.

This, then, is the soundtrack to my childhood: the screams of men, the soothing lullabies of my mother. The strange noises I embrace in the night.

At the bottom of the garden, beyond the boundary of the last hedge, is a narrow river. I sometimes go there to play with my dolls. It's very quiet and no one really bothers me there. Very few people even know where it is. I take Sally and Francine with me and we sit on the embankment and watch the quick fish glide through the reeds. Sally doesn't bend very well, so I have to force her legs back as far as they'll go before she can sit on the grass and watch the river without falling in. Francine is much more flexible; she sits beside Sally and stares at the water. They listen patiently and we talk for hours until it gets dark; sometimes we talk about running away. Or hiding at the bottom of the river where no one can find us; where not even Mother would be able to drag us back.

I sit on the bank and take off Francine's clothes. The plastic skin underneath is hard and pink. I hold my own hand next to the doll's chest. Francine's skin doesn't look at all like mine; it looks like weathered stone, all hard and smooth. I press a finger into my cheek, worried that it might have changed; that it might not be as soft and yielding as I remember. But my finger sinks in to the skin just fine and I continue undressing the doll.

Once I've removed all of Francine's clothes, I fold them just as Mother taught me and place them in a neat pile on the grass. I hold the doll over the edge of the bank and let Francine's golden hair fall into the river. It looks beautiful, like a cloud of yellow paint mixing with the running water. I imagine my own hair doing that and think again about burying myself in the dark sludge of the riverbed, as my hair grows and grows until it takes on a life of its own, a golden weed floating free among the silver fins of the fish.

"Hello, Elizabeth."

I glance up, startled to hear a voice out here that isn't my own. Especially one calling me by the name my mother favours, instead of the one I prefer.

Standing twenty feet away are two girls. They look immaculate. They have the same face with one alarming exception: the one on the right, Penny, has a small scar beneath her left eye. The other one, Genna, is perfect. She is the girl I have seen over and over again on the television and in the movies, and on the glossy covers of magazines. She is the kind of child every adult adores and every child secretly resents. I sometimes wonder what her sister thinks, late at night, when Genna is fast asleep; when Penny's scar, in the hollow darkness, starts to throb.

"My name is Ellie," I say softly. "Only my mother calls me Elizabeth."

"I'm not at all sure that matters very much. Are you, Gen?" Penny shoots a smile in my direction, but it's colourless and insincere. When they stand together like this, drawing attention to the biological quirk that has shaped them, I often think how disturbing it is to see two people, where really there should only be one. It isn't too much of a stretch to imagine that Penny is merely an imperfect clone of Genna, the two girls living exactly the same life.

I hold my breath as they suddenly notice Francine.

"Is it dolly's bath day?" Genna says, laughing.

I say nothing, knowing from past experience that I'm damned either way.

"What's its name?" Penny says. "They always have names, don't they, Gen?"

Genna nods and they both wait, watching me shift on the embankment with steady, defiant eyes.

"Just Alice," I say, feeling uncomfortable. "I call her Alice." There's no way I'd ever tell them Francine's real name; they'd spoil it forever.

"That's a bitch's name," Genna says. "I know lots of bitches named Alice. Don't you, Pen?"

Penny nods and tries to stifle a laugh. "Bitches and cows," she says. "Every single Alice I know."

I pull Francine from the river and gently squeeze water from her hair.

"How many do you know?" I say.

Genna looks at Penny and then turns to me.

"It doesn't matter how many I know," she says, taking several steps in my direction. "The point is, I know a bitch when I see one, *Elizabeth*, and I'm looking at one right now. A crazy little girl bitch who still plays with her dolly and washes its fucking hair in the river."

She breaks into a run and, before I can react, has snatched Francine out of my hands.

I break into a sweat and run wet fingers through my unkempt hair.

"Give her back. You shouldn't touch her. She's my mother's."

Penny has raced up to join her sister and the two of them are throwing Francine to one another through the air, knowing that eventually I'll be drawn stupidly—and inevitably—into the middle.

"Look," Penny says. "She's flying!"

The two girls are laughing hard now. They throw Francine high over my head and I jump and reach out my arms to try and catch her. When I look up I see Francine spinning through a blue, cloudless sky, her wet hair trailing across an unchanging face.

Sometimes Francine is dropped and I consider fighting for her while she's still on the ground; but I know that if one sister is threatened, the other will automatically respond. I'm in no mood to have to explain away a cut lip and a bruised face to Mother. Not again; it just doesn't seem worth the effort anymore.

I leave them to their silly game and take a step or two away from the bank. The throwing of the doll instantly stops. Genna looks across at me and smiles. She holds Francine up to her ear.

"Little Alice here says that, after all that exercise, she fancies a swim." She and Penny exchange a knowing glance. "What do you think, Elizabeth? The ugly bitch won't drown, will she?"

I say nothing; I stand and observe Genna's unkindness, failing to understand how it works. For a brief moment it occurs to me that I could charge forward and tip both of them into the river, Genna and the doll. Penny would surely be too preoccupied saving her sister to consider how best to exact revenge; unless the throbbing of the scar kicked in and she watched in silent relief as the perfect version of herself gently floated away.

When she next looks up the moment is gone. Genna has clearly tired of the afternoon's entertainment and both girls are ready to move on.

"Deep breath," Genna says, laughing. She throws Francine into the river and she and Penny walk back the way they came, giggling and calling me names over their shoulder.

I ignore them and instead watch Francine drift along the speeding current towards a new future. She is quickly passing out of sight. I think about trying to rescue her, but then realise she has been granted an opportunity to break free; a chance to become one with the deep-flowing waters of the river, constantly moving, never settling in the same place twice.

Swim fast, my friend. Swim as hard as you can.

I wonder why I don't feel a greater sense of excitement, and then it hits. I am envious. My doll is floating away down the river and I feel like weeping. I desperately want it to be me.

I sit in my bedroom, trying to avoid Mother. She's being particularly loving today and it makes me feel uncomfortable. She has that look in her eye, the one that means *I'm trying to do right by you so pay attention and be bloody grateful for it while it lasts.* The best thing to do when she gets like this is to lay low; eventually her sense of responsibility will pass and she'll return to her normal, abstracted self. I feel more at ease when she's preoccupied with other things; when her attention turns to me, it's like I've wandered into the remorseless gaze of one of those creatures from *War of the Worlds*. No matter how still I sit, sooner or later she'll sense my presence. On a bad day she'll start asking about school; on a really bad day she'll start talking about her 'men friends', the losers who cry into her bosom as they vainly attempt to hide the mysterious bulge inside their trousers.

One of my men friends lost his wife in a terrible car accident. Had to be cut out of the vehicle, he said. They scraped her face off the dashboard, for heaven's sake. Can you imagine such a thing, Elizabeth? An accident so bad it strips you of your identity. The torment that poor man's been through. I still can't believe it. No face!

I close my eyes when Mother talks like this, knowing it can rumble on for an entire afternoon. The notion of leaving one's identity behind does not sound like such a terrible one to me, though if I admitted this to Mother she'd think I was baiting her; would no doubt find a way of using my confession to remind me of how selfish I've become.

Not everything is about you, Elizabeth. God forbid we should go five minutes without falling off our stools over something you've said!

When she slips into one of these moods, I can barely

understand a word she says. She seems to speak mostly for effect, and always to an invisible audience. When it grows tiresome, I usually just tuck myself away in a darkened corner of the house, and wait for enough time to have passed for Mother to forget about how terrible I am.

I stand up and move across the room to the window. In the adjacent garden I can see the boy. I often see him out there, stripped to the waist, carving wild animals from blocks of wood. I don't know his name, so I have christened him Joseph; a good name for a carpenter, I think. Like me, he lives alone with his mother, but we have no contact with them. Mother is not well-liked in the community, probably because of the service she provides for her 'men friends', and none of the other women talk to her. They cross the road when they see her coming, and Mother lifts her chin and grips my hand hard. She tells me secret stuff about them, stuff she has been told in confidence by the men.

I look through the window and watch Joseph's hands working gracefully across the contours of the wood. He is carving a tiger. He has smoothed out the long line of its back and it looks like the boy's own, pale and sleek and untouched. If he knows I am watching him, he shows no sign of it; he has never once looked up. His focus is always on the animals trapped inside the wood that he slowly releases with his hands.

That boy looks like trouble. Look at his eyes; too close together. Wouldn't trust him for a minute, and neither should you. As for his mother! Don't get me started, Elizabeth. I could tell you a few stories about her. Likes her liquor, that one. Or so I'm led to believe...

Mother is *'led to believe'* more than is good for her, and I often wonder how she and her 'men friends' stumble on to topics like the woman next door. Mother assures me that it is all part of the healing process, but I'm not convinced. It sounds to me like Mother is using the men to gain an advantage as she wages a secret, unwinnable war.

I risk a further look at Joseph as he runs a hand over yet another finished piece. He is surrounded by flakes of wood; he has dust in his hair. But the tiger is finally free.

I like to walk around the village early in the morning when it's quiet, usually before Mother makes me trudge to school. I see things that lots of people are too busy or too stupid to observe. I sit on top of Sealer's Ridge and watch the sun rise over the distant hills. It peeks over the horizon and then hauls itself up, and it's suddenly so bright I'm not even sure what I'm looking at anymore. It's like my memory of everything has been wiped.

The morning always smells so fresh, so new; when I draw breath my lungs feel cold and tight, inflated with a tiny piece of the miracle, as though for a single moment in what I know will be a dismal day, I've been blessed.

I follow the same path that I tread every day, carrying three slices of cold toast in a Tupperware container and a small thermos of black coffee. When I reach Langton's farm I clamber onto the gate and squint into the sun. Harry is on the far side of the field, driving his plough through the dark earth. He sees me and waves. I wave back. Within five minutes he has ground to a halt and I watch his dark outline lumbering across the heavy ground towards me. He greets me with a gap-toothed smile.

"Morning, Ellie. How's the world treating you?"

"Same as always, Harry. Like I kicked it in the teeth and deserve payback."

He laughs and swings himself onto the gate.

"I like that. Reckon I'll use it later in the pub."

"That's okay," I say. "I stole it off the TV."

He laughs again and holds out his hands. I hand over the thermos of coffee and the container. He loves his toast cold and hard, so I pop it in the freezer for half an hour before I set off. He says it reminds him of the toast he used to eat at an old B&B his dad used to take him to when he was a kid. I tried a piece once and it nearly made me sick; it was like eating buttered cardboard.

He undoes the thermos and pours some of the coffee into the cup. It steams darkly in the morning air.

"You," he says "are an angel. Have I told you that?"

I smile. "A few times, Harry. But I like hearing it."

He undoes the container and starts eating the cold toast. In between each mouthful he takes a hot slug of black coffee to help wash it down.

"How's your mother? Still crushing the life out of you?"

I look away, a little ashamed of the portrait I must have painted of my own mother. Not all of the things I've confessed to Harry are entirely true.

"It's not all that bad," I say. "She takes pretty good care of me really. Just a bit too protective."

Harry nods his head and crunches on the toast. "All parents are the same. There's something in your blood and theirs that changes everything the minute you're born. That's the way it's always been."

I think about this for a moment and watch him as he sits on the gate and eats his breakfast. *Something in the blood that changes everything.* It makes me feel uneasy, as though Harry has just diagnosed an illness that I'll never be able to shake. The idea that Mother and I share the same blood is also a notion that alarms me.

I sit watching Harry, admiring his heavy hands and the dark lines etched into his face. He looks a lot like the earth itself, rugged and deeply furrowed, as though working the land has slowly transformed him into its living, breathing twin. I reach a hand to my face and touch my skin; it feels smooth and cool, nothing like the landscape that stretches before me. It is without distinction, flat and clear; more like the sky than the earth.

"Have you seen your friend?" Harry says, polishing off the toast and wiping crumbs from around his mouth.

He means the boy, Joseph. The one I sometimes watch. I nod, feeling a little guilty. I told Harry he looks like a young version of him because both of them work with their hands.

"Was he carving again?"

I pause, thinking about the animal the boy created out of wood. "I think he's more talented than he realises," I say.

"Most young people are, Ellie. They just need a little encouragement, a push in the right direction to set them off."

I feel a stab of disappointment. If I have a talent it's keeping a very low profile. I'm not good at anything. Not a single, miserable thing.

I jump from the gate and land awkwardly. My heart is racing; it occurs to me that if I don't leave soon I might cry.

"I have to go," I tell Harry. I reach up for the thermos and the Tupperware container and he gently places them in my hands.

"Same time tomorrow?" he says.

I nod, then turn and walk away. Perhaps this is my talent, I think: an uncanny ability to always feel empty inside.

The man awoke at the same time as always: 6.45am. His first thought was erratic and unclear, the fragment of a lost dream, most of which had already been broken up and dispersed deep inside his head. What was left was an image of a small child wearing his face, rushing towards an endless darkness; an image that fell away without leaving even the faintest imprint as soon as he opened his eyes.

He threw back the covers and slid his feet into cold slippers. They felt soft, reminding him of the deep pile rug his parents used to own; he would run his bare feet through the fibres of the rug every night before his father told him it was time to go to bed.

He walked to the bathroom and washed and shaved in hot water. As usual, the soap felt unpleasant in his hands, like a living creature squirming to escape, and it was at this point that any last vestige of sleep disappeared for good. He rinsed, brushed his teeth and dabbed himself dry with a towel.

He looked at himself in the mirror. His face was too long or too narrow or too small, he could never quite decide. He gritted his teeth together and thought they looked tiny, especially when surrounded by his large, rubber lips. When he bit into things he sometimes wondered what the hell was going on inside his mouth.

He ran a comb through his hair and smiled into the mirror. He looked presentable. His eyes looked tired and old, but everyone looked the same these days. It was getting harder to disguise the fact that he felt a thousand years old; that ignoring the blood and thunder of each passing week never really altered a thing. He stared hard into the mirror and realised that the man he imagined himself to be had been ambushed by someone else: a cold-eyed, stretch-marked creature that bore only a mild resemblance to the man he remembered. He tried on another smile and felt ill, wondering how long he'd be forced to keep such a wretched affectation in place.

He left the bathroom and walked downstairs to the kitchen. As he passed the front door, he collected the news-

paper that was resting on the welcome mat and folded it underneath his arm. It was the one luxury he allowed himself at the start of every day. Fifteen minutes alone with The Independent; *an opportunity to acquaint himself with the horrors of the outside world.*

He entered the kitchen and placed the newspaper on the table. He spent a moment thinking about the coming day, considering the same possibility he always considered: whether this would be the day when he finally broke with routine and stumbled nervously towards something new.

He filled the kettle with water and made himself a cup of black coffee. At the same time he toasted two slices of bread, buttered them, and took both the toast and the coffee to the kitchen table. He sat down, opened the newspaper and ate his breakfast whilst reading about the latest economic downturn across the EU.

If the start of the man's day was at all unusual, it was only in so much as he had no idea what might happen once he stepped outside the front door. Everything else seemed perfectly run-of-the-mill; a pattern repeated in thousands of houses across the land, where single, middle-aged men were shaving, drinking coffee, reading the newspaper and eating toast.

Fifteen minutes after opening The Independent *he folded it and slid it inside his briefcase. He placed his breakfast pots by the sink and wiped crumbs from his mouth with a faded dishtowel. He pulled on his coat and moved down the hall towards the front door. He hovered for a moment by the oak cabinet and stared at the fruit bowl. It looked full; he must have restocked it during the night. He smiled and admired the wide variety of colours through the glass. He felt good; the day had started without any bad thoughts. Proof, perhaps, that he was capable of guiding himself away from the dark.*

He opened the front door, waved to Mrs Freeman across the road, and picked two kumquats from the bowl as he left.

I visit my grandparents twice a week, and on the way I like to take a detour and head towards the abandoned mill that sits on the ridge, overlooking the old part of the village. Grampa says it used to be a paper mill, but refuses to be drawn on the details; whenever I try to ask him about it he changes the subject. Nan says it should have been knocked down years ago. She told me Grampa's still angry that the mill closed back in the 60s, when a lot of people in the village relied on it for work. If you stand in Nan's kitchen and stare out the window while you're washing up or making a cup of tea, the mill watches you from on top of the ridge; Nan calls it an eyesore. I've noticed she never looks directly at it when she's working at the sink.

I approach my grandparents' house from the rear, travelling across Harry's freshly-ploughed field, and climb across the ridge towards the mill. It always looks dark, no matter what time of day it is, as though the brickwork is reluctant to step into the light. I forget how big it is until the building is towering over me; it's like staring at the bones of a dinosaur, the skeleton of the mill pressed into the rock of the village forever, despised by everyone in the community but me. Its emptiness used to frighten me, but now I realise it is this very quality that attracts me the most. I enjoy standing in the heart of the disused mill listening to the sound of nothing. I look at the broken windows and the imposing machinery and feel like I've stumbled into an exotic dimension, a world far away from Mother and the terrible twins, and the tiny cruelties I am expected to endure at school.

I push my way towards the rotted boards that lead down

to the basement and ease past the weeds and the broken glass. I shove the boards to one side and clamber down into the darkness. I don't really like this part of the mill, but it appears to be the only way in. The basement is pitch-black; I always get the sense when I'm in here that the things I should be worried about the most are lurking just out of reach, waiting for me to lose my footing in the dark. It feels like all the light has been used up; like the people who abandoned the mill all those years ago stored its wickedest secrets in this very room and then fled, praying that they'd never have any reason to return.

I pass quickly through the darkness and climb the stone steps towards the main operational level of the mill. Dim light seeps in through the high windows, the glass panes smashed an eternity ago by children who have since become adults, who now warn their own kids to stay away from the place. The floor itself is huge, dominated by rows of unmanned machines, many of which have been stripped down to reveal cogs and gears that haven't turned in over four decades. When I first came here these monstrous engines terrified me; I could see leaking batteries and wires and broken valves, and I wondered what kind of sickness could possibly have befallen them. Every piece of equipment that could be salvaged had been painstakingly removed, leaving only the heavy outer shells crouching in the dim light, the metal joints soundlessly yielding to rust.

Now, as I walk down the aisles, I find the presence of the dead machines reassuring, as though their final function is to watch over me as I prowl through the redundant mill. I think about all those who have been here before me: first the workers, their puny arms frantically operating levers and gears, their overalls dark with oil and sweat; then the thieves, working late into the night to bring the place crashing to its knees; then the kids, exploring every forgotten corner, delighting in their good fortune as the cooling shadows spread across the ghostly anatomy of the mill.

I feel at home here. I suppose that's why I return so frequently, using my grandparents as a cover story whenever Mother starts to wonder where I am.

It's not healthy, you know, visiting old folk so much. All they want to talk about is themselves. You ought to be mixing with people your own age, Elizabeth. Girls from school. I don't understand why you never invite your friends round to the house. It's like you're ashamed of me, or something . . .

I've heard this song before, and as soon as Mother starts singing it I smile and turn away, refusing to be sucked in to her dysfunctional world where everything is in some way related to her. It saddens me to think that my own mother knows so little about me. I can't remember ever talking about a friend from school, because I don't think I've ever really had one. Not properly. When I was younger, some of the kids used to play *near* me; but as we grew up even this minor intimacy was lost. We became more self-aware and something in the way they responded to me changed. I've no idea what it was. I don't suppose I'll ever know. I was just different. I didn't dress like them; I didn't talk like them; I didn't think like them. I suppose they just saw something in me that they didn't understand, and that was enough. From that moment on I became invisible: the girl nobody ever dared go near.

When Mother starts questioning me about friends or wonders aloud why I always seem so difficult to get along with, I want to scream in her face and tell her exactly what it's like to be the only schoolgirl standing alone in the yard.

They hate me! Can't you see that? Those girls you're so desperate for me to bring home, they treat me like shit. Every one of them. They spit on me and pull my hair and trip me up when I walk past; if I fall down, they kick me in the stomach and call me a whore. Those girls you like so much, Mother, call me Lizzie Rawcunt and say I fuck animals for fun. Are they really the kind of girls you want me to bring back to the house . . . ?

I try to imagine what it must be like having a friend, but the notion is so alien to me I can't even begin to visualise it. I'm not used to seeing another girl's face without a snarl of contempt or a grimace etched into it. The most I ever expect is for their cruelly wandering eye to alight upon me and then to move on, as if I barely exist. When this occurs I stand relieved, not even questioning for a minute why this entire moral line might be wrong. This is simply the measure of a good day; I consider their failure to notice me a blessing, a singular gift, for which I'm likely to remain thankful until the next girl comes along, delivering the next unkindness. I want to howl until Mother understands: *This is what it's like being me.*

I stop for a moment, surrounded by the hulls of neglected machines, and enjoy the silence. No cruelty, no chanting, no petty torment; just the soundless company of the lengthening shadows. In its prime this place would have been a heaving workhouse, the equipment so noisy it would have been impossible for the men operating them to talk over the thrashing motors. Not so now; instead there is a perfect stillness about the mill that leaves me breathless with gratitude. Here, at last, is a place where I am at peace; where I never feel unwelcome and where the whispered threats of my enemies go unheard.

I smile at my good fortune and make my way towards the large open space at the far end of the mill. I inhale the pulpy smell of chemicals and wood that still seems to emanate from the brick walls, and approach the battered folding table that I set up here months ago having reclaimed it from Mother's shed. I also found a small wooden crate in one of the outhouses, which I use as a stool. I sometimes come here and sit at the table, and quietly draw the machines. I try and picture them the way they were: powerful, gears grinding, the great engines roaring through the night. I prefer to think of them this way; they feel more alive, and I wonder how close my drawings are to the heat and intensity of the real thing. When I'm here I can sense the sweat and the labour and the love; it's a kind of happiness that I've never encountered before. It makes me feel giddy with relief, as though I have earned the right to just a fraction of this happiness, too. When I close my eyes the mill belongs to me. I am safe here. Nothing in the world has the power to take that away.

I edge closer to the table and realise there is something resting on its scuffed surface. I stop dead in my tracks, unable to take another step. I think I am holding my breath, but I can't be sure. The axis of the world in which I live has suddenly *tipped*. I squint my eyes and look again, wondering if I've made a mistake, but the table and the object set upon it remain the same. I want to touch it, but I'm afraid, and instead I stand and stare, wondering if it's been placed here just for me: a carved wooden tiger, deep in the heart of the mill.

Later that night I watch from my window to see if Joseph will appear in his garden. The moonlight washes across the yard. I feel warm inside. My mind is hot and stuffy, and none of my thoughts seem to make any sense. I wonder what he's doing in the house next door. I imagine him carving in his room and secretly thinking of me. I feel sick. I hold on to the wooden tiger for dear life.

The following morning Mother is up early. She is wearing her work clothes and the kitchen table holds a wicker basket, two pairs of gloves and a pair of long-handled wire cutters. We are obviously running low on cash.

"Get moving, Missy," she says. "We have work to do."

"I don't think I can. I don't feel so good."

Mother takes one look at me and places the back of her hand against my forehead.

"Nonsense. You're just dandy. Now hurry up and get changed. Those blackberries won't pick themselves."

I sigh, failing to understand why we have to play out this ridiculous self-deception every single time. I know the drill by now. Blackberry picking is Mother's affectionate euphemism for stealing copper wire from the train track behind our house. It isn't altogether untrue, I suppose. We work in tandem; me picking blackberries and keeping watch, Mother stripping copper from the tracks.

"I don't want to do it anymore," I say. "It's too dangerous. Someone could get hurt."

"No one ever got cancer picking blackberries," Mother says. She puts the wire cutters and the gloves inside the wicker basket and looks surprised when she realises I haven't moved. "Get your jam pots, Elizabeth, and stop dragging your heels. We can't afford to lollygag, you know."

I don't know what this means, but it sounds uncomfortable. I resolve to look it up in the dictionary as soon as Mother frees me from my obligation. I walk into the utility room, shrug on my overalls, and trudge off to collect the jam pots from the shed. When I return Mother is all set to go. She hands me a pair of gloves from the basket and ushers me out of the door.

We stride down the back garden towards the narrow gap

in the hedge. On the other side is the river in which I used to wash Francine's hair, and beyond this is the railway line that my Mother occasionally raids to supplement her meagre income. We walk alongside the river for about half a mile and arrive at a wooden footbridge, which we silently cross. Another few hundred yards and we scramble up the railway embankment to the deserted track. Mother assures me that the line has been out of service for several years, but whenever we stand on the wooden sleepers I always feel a mounting sense of unease. Looking down the line as the track vanishes into the horizon, I imagine I can feel a distant vibration travelling from my feet to my racing heart. It is too easy to picture Mother being atomised by an oncoming train, her sprayed blood mixing with the blackberry juice I have unwittingly smeared across my hands and my face and my clothes.

I stand on the track and look along its length as Mother gets to work. It's still early in the morning and there is a thin trailing mist creeping along the line. The air is cold and my hands are trembling, but the gloves smell of mould and I refuse to put them on. The glass jam pots are jangling against my leg.

I look across at Mother and watch as she bends low to the track. She is an efficient, meticulous worker; she knows exactly how to get things done. Her hair falls across her eyes and she snakes it away with a gloved hand. She is breathing like a steam engine, keeping a steady rhythm, blowing hard as she works the muscles in her shoulders and arms. The wire cutters move easily, harvesting the crimped copper wire connected to the metal joints of the track. Each piece is about two foot long. Twenty of them will net Mother a hundred pounds from Gasdin's Scrapyard. If we're lucky a month might pass before we're reduced to having to do it all again.

Mother stops for a moment and looks up. I haven't moved; I watch a bead of perspiration form between her eyes and slide along the slope of her nose like a tear.

"Why the hell ain't you picking them damn blackberries?" she says, scowling at me, her speech coarse with anger. "You're not even trying. Get those jam pots moving, Missy!"

I move towards the bramble bush growing wild by the side of the line and start filling the glass jars with blackberries. The mist grovels in the dirt around my feet. A dozen yards away Mother fills the wicker basket with stolen copper she has lifted from the track. As I pick the fruit I notice my fingers darkening; my hands feel heavy with their blood. For every three I pick, I pop at least two into my mouth. They taste sweet, like something forbidden, and I automatically think of Joseph and the wooden tiger I have stashed away in my room. I pick a handful of blackberries and squash them in my palm. When I open my hand, they look like clotted black tumours. I think of the twins tormenting me and the imperfection on Penny's face. That single scar running beneath her left eye. A pale question mark, hanging there for everyone to see.

I wipe my stained hands on my overalls and continue picking. The jam pots are almost full to the brim.

Mother looks over to make sure I'm doing my bit. "You're not wearing your gloves," she says. "You'll be red raw in the morning."

I close my eyes, hearing the girls at school chanting *Lizzie Rawcunt!* over and over again until I find a quiet place where I can weep without interruption.

"I don't need them," I say. "I like the feel of the berries in my hands."

"If you have a bad reaction, don't come crying to me about it." She turns her attention back to the track and, when she's not looking, I stick out my tongue. I'm not brave enough yet to do anything else, but in my head I call her a *miserable old cow* and feel my cheeks burn. It's about as far as I permit myself to go.

"You see anyone?" Mother asks.

I look up and down the embankment and see nothing but ragged trails of mist. Further along the line is an old semaphore signal. At some point bored children have pelted it with blackberries; it is heavily stained with dried black juice.

"All clear," I say.

Mother returns to her labour, patiently working along the track and clipping the copper fibres. I watch my chilled breath ghost away in the morning air.

"There must be easier ways of making money than this," I say. Even to my untrained eye it looks like an awful lot of effort for very little return.

Mother stops what she's doing and places the wire cutters on the ground.

"I suppose there must," she says. "Do you happen to know any of them?"

I look down at my jam pots. "We could collect blackberries and sell them door-to-door. We could make jams and pies for the village."

Mother stares at me. "Good grief, Elizabeth. We're trying to make money, not friends. You'd have me up to my armpits in jam juice all day, wouldn't you?"

I turn away, trying to picture Mother in the kitchen with a rolling pin and flour-white hands.

"How broke are we?" I ask.

Mother picks up the cutters. "We have enough to get by," she says, "so mind your beeswax."

This is Mother's stock response to any question she feels uncomfortable answering. She knows it annoys me. Irritated, I fire a shot across the bows.

"We could always ask Nan and Grampa to help," I say.

Mother's eyes turn dark. "And why, pray, would we want to do that?"

I open my arms to embrace the absurdity of where we are. "So we don't have to do this," I say, somewhat glibly.

"The last thing I want is to be in debt to those two old crows. Maybe one day, when you're older, you'll understand."

Somehow I doubt that. Mother's relationship with her own parents is a complicated one, and I still haven't quite figured out the root cause. I think it has something to do with their disapproval of Mother's relationship with my biological father. When he ran off and abandoned her during her pregnancy, all their previous fears were confirmed.

I move along the bush, continuing to pick blackberries, most of which I eat as both the jam pots are already full. I place them on the ground and look along the line of the mist-covered embankment. Half a dozen yards to my left, just visible in the cold light, I see a small paw protruding from the brambles. I move closer and pull on my gloves. I lift the belly of the shrub from the ground and lean in for a closer look. A dead badger, turned grey with dirt from its nocturnal run, is lying half-buried in the broken earth. There is a hole in its stomach where something has attacked it. The wound looks hard and red. I stare at it for a moment and feel a great sense of sadness. Its black eyes are open and the dead creature watches me, seeing no further threat. I lower the bush and leave the animal in peace, but the empty gaze of those black eyes stays with me. I have seen it before, that look, and the realisation fills me with dread: the badger's vacant stare is exactly like my own.

*T*he man had been driving the same roads for the last hour, feeling lost and alone, the bad thoughts trailing him like smoke. He had kept them at bay for most of the afternoon, even when he had found himself reaching into his coat pocket to caress the fruit; now, with the low light of the evening sun blinding him through the windscreen, the bad thoughts were leaking out. They were showing him things he didn't want to see.

He drove on for another ten minutes and felt suffocated by the heat inside the car. He was starting to sweat; he could feel the rash on his neck rubbing against the fibres of his shirt. His sense of claustrophobia was heightening and he could feel the cramped space beginning to close in on him. The bad thoughts told him he had to stop. If he pulled over, he could breathe in fresh air; he could reach inside his pocket and feel the soothing skin of the fruit.

He indicated left and pulled the car onto an access road he knew well. It ran adjacent to the local park. He climbed out of the car, took a deep, comforting breath, and sank his hands into his coat pockets. They quickly found the rounded flesh of the kumquats; he sighed and closed his eyes.

On the back of his lids, tethered to the darkness, the children were already waiting. They were lined up, smiling at him, their faces perfect, their bodies angular and crude, like the figures of stick men. They were watching him expectantly and he smiled at their patience; they were waiting to touch the fruit.

He opened his eyes and moved purposefully along the access road to the back entrance of the park. He was feeling calmer and his breathing had returned to normal. His cheeks were rosy in the cold air as though he'd just completed a leisurely run.

He went to the oak tree that he liked and watched the children pass by as the bad thoughts drifted away. They weren't bad anymore; they were just part of who he was. He took the kumquats from his pockets and held them in his hand. They nestled in his palm like strange orange eggs. The colour was seductive; it was always the colour that first drew them in.

After several minutes a small girl wearing a grey blazer and a navy skirt approached him. She was carrying a pink Peppa Pig backpack. Her white socks were rolled down to her ankles; she had dark scabs on her knees.

"What are they?" she said. "They look pretty."

"These?" the man said. "These are called kumquats. They're a special kind of fruit. They taste like sunlight."

He bit into one; the orange skin split and juice dripped around the corners of his mouth.

"Here," he said. "Try one."

He handed one to the little girl. She paused for a moment, undecided, and then accepted it. She bit into the bright orange flesh and looked surprised.

"Well?"

"Sour," the girl said, taking another bite and smiling.

The man watched, mesmerised.

"They grow on a very special tree at the end of that road," he said. He pointed away from the park. "Want to see?"

She stared at him for a moment, then nodded.

The man held out his hand; tentatively, the little girl took it.

I knock on my grandparents' back door and walk in, just as I always do.

"Only me," I shout, so as not to alarm them. "I've made you some blackberry jam."

"Lovely," Nan says from the front room. "Leave it on the

side. We can have jam butties for tea." She sounds a little preoccupied and I place the jar of jam on the kitchen table and walk through into the lounge. Grampa has his leg hoisted onto the saggy leather pouffe that they've had since the war. Nan is changing his dressing; the wound is shockingly pink against the rest of his pale left leg. They have given up hoping that the NHS will successfully treat Grampa's injury and Nan is using maggot debridement therapy to try and speed up the healing process. The accident occurred nearly five weeks ago and his leg still looks horrific. The impact of the crash and the burst radiator did most of the damage, though Grampa insists that the meddling junior doctors made it significantly worse.

"You squeamish?" Grampa says. "'Cause this ain't very pretty."

"I'm fine, Grampa. I've seen stuff like this before." I picture the hole in the stomach of the dead badger and then stare at the seeping pus in Grampa's leg. I can't decide which is worse.

"Grampa's right, Ellie. This might not be appropriate. Your mother would pitch a fit."

All the more reason to watch then, I think.

"It's okay, Nan. Mother doesn't need to know, does she? Besides, I'm interested in this stuff. You can teach me how it works." Nan used to be a nurse before she retired; she says this is how she knows for sure that the NHS is a hotbed of incompetence.

She sighs and pats the sofa. "Sit down then, lass," she says. "I've work to do."

I take a seat beside her and watch as she disinfects the wound. Nan has already told me a bit about maggot debridement therapy. She says it's called MDT and is a tried and trusted method to aid healing. The maggots sit in the open wound and eat only the dead and infected tissue.

They kill all bacteria and remove the source of infection; it's like having tiny surgeons working on the surface of the wound, making the area safe again so that a full recovery can begin.

I lean in as Nan works on Grampa's leg, fascinated and appalled in equal measure. She has prepared Grampa's wound and now reaches over for a small Perspex tub. Air holes have been punched into the top. The label on the side reads, *Medical Maggots: use within 24 hours of delivery. 250-500 larvae.* The lid is secured by an adhesive strip that reads: *Sterile. Do not use if seal is broken.*

Nan breaks off the tape and pours a liberal sprinkling of the maggots onto Grampa's leg. I pull a face, wondering what it must feel like. I picture the badger again and go cold; imagine the dead creature with its own army of maggots relentlessly picking at its corpse.

"What kind of maggots are they, Nan?" I say to try and take my mind off the badger.

Nan affixes a rectangle of nylon netting over the maggots and holds it in place with four strips of medical tape. I watch the tiny creatures wriggling around in Grampa's flesh, their pale bodies already getting to work on the black ridge of skin around the wound.

"These are specially prepared medical maggots," Nan said. "They're green blow fly. Pretty yucky, huh?"

I see Grampa grinning and I smile, though in truth I am starting to feel a little sick.

"Aren't you afraid one of the maggots might bury itself under your skin and start crawling around?" I ask.

Grampa frowns. "I am now," he says. He looks at Nan for clarification. A small part of me is secretly pleased that I have wiped Grampa's smug grin from his face.

Nan smiles. "These maggots are incredibly smart, Ellie. When all the dead tissue has been eaten away they'll prepare to leave the body. They won't bury themselves in or feed on healthy tissue. They're too clever by far."

Grampa looks relieved and I feel slightly cheated, as though Nan has shattered some of the terrifying mystique.

"What if they turn into flies?" I say, trying to resurrect some of Grampa's doubts. "They'll be trapped in there, laying eggs."

The blood drains from Grampa's face and he looks to Nan again for reassurance.

"Nothing like that will happen, Silly Susan," she says, cuffing me gently round the head. "Medical grade maggots are sterile. Besides which, they aren't mature enough yet to reproduce. Now stop making mischief and hand me that dressing."

She points to a gauze pad on the floor and I retrieve it for her and hand it across. She places it over the mesh and tapes it in place.

"Maggots need oxygen, Ellie, so all the dressings I apply have to be porous. We also need to make sure that any liquefied tissue can easily drain away."

"Why do they need the net?" I say. "It's like they're trapped in there."

"They're perfectly fine," Nan says. "The net is to stop the maggots from migrating. As soon as they're full, or when there's no more dead tissue to eat, the maggots will try and crawl away as quickly as possible. A bit like you, Ellie, after your dinner when you're desperate to leave the table to watch TV."

I smile at Nan, deciding that she must have made a wonderful nurse. I could listen to her stories all day; more importantly, I think she'd be happy to talk, even to me.

"What happens if one of them bites you, Grampa, when it should be chomping on the dead tissue?"

Grampa's skin colour drops a shade; he is clearly no

longer enjoying my company. I can see in his eyes that he would rather I be anywhere but here.

"That's not possible, is it Nell?"

Another smile from Nan. "What do you think?" she says. She turns her attention back to me. "Maggots don't have teeth, they have mandibles called mouthhooks. They have rough bumps on their body that pull away the dead tissue and then the mouthhooks do the rest of the work. It's perfectly painless."

"Can you feel them, Grampa?"

"Only when they get a bit fatter and they crawl over some of the exposed nerves," he says, recovering his composure. "At the minute, lass, your Nan keeps the entire leg numb with medication. And bloody grateful I am for it, too."

Nan applies the last layers of dressing and then binds the whole of Grampa's lower leg in a medical stocking.

"There," she says. "All done."

She secures the lid of the maggot tub and takes it into the kitchen as Grampa tries to make himself comfortable in his armchair. He picks up the newspaper and buries his head in yesterday's misery. I follow Nan into the kitchen, impressed with both her skill and the depth of her knowledge; I try to imagine what the maggots are doing in the newly-sterilised darkness of Grampa's leg.

"Where do you keep them?" I ask.

"In the fridge," she says. "Right next to the butter and the jam."

I pull a face and make a vomiting noise. Nan laughs. I laugh too and throw my arms around her waist. I bury my head in her bosom and close my eyes; she smells of disinfectant and scented soap. I listen to her heartbeat through her clothes.

Later that night, I am awakened by a single scream, short and full of grief, that draws me from sleep and sets my heart racing in the dark. I sit up, anticipating something more. A full-blooded howl, perhaps; or a blubbering collapse as Mother patiently strokes away the pain. But there is nothing. No more anguish; no more screams. Just silence, and the lingering sweetness of the night.

I climb out of bed and pull on my dressing gown. Even in the dark I can see the faint outline of Spongebob clowning around with Patrick. It is a hand-me-down from one of Nan's friends; the sleep smell of the last owner has been forever embedded in the nap.

I stumble from my room and walk quietly to the top of the stairs. I can hear Mother whispering something to the grieving man she has invited into the house. It leaves me feeling hot and mildly embarrassed, as though I have been caught ogling a train wreck. There is a metallic taste in my mouth, a combination of sleep and self-loathing; the better part of me knows that I should turn around and go straight back to bed.

But I don't. I press on. I walk halfway down the stairs, lower myself onto a step, and peer between the wooden spindles. The door to the lounge is half-open; I can see directly into the room. Mother is sitting on the sofa. Lying down, with his head in her lap, is Harry. He is moaning softly and crying. He is naked from the waist down and Mother is touching him; he looks ludicrously big. She is slowly stroking him, telling him everything is going to be fine. Harry has his eyes closed. He is whispering the name of his dead wife.

I hold my breath and try to look away, but I can't. The sight of Mother attending to Harry's grief in this way is like a nail in my heart. I want to scream at her to stop, but the realisation that she is actually helping to heal him in this way is making me want to pluck out my own eyes in shame. I think of the maggots on Grampa's leg as I watch Mother whisper in Harry's ear, soothing lullabies that compel him to draw a hand across his face and weep.

I picture him sitting beside me on the wooden gate of the field saying: *How's your mother? Still crushing the life out of you?* and I watch Mother's hand with mounting horror as it begins to knead and caress and *crush*.

I force myself to look away and run back to my bedroom, feeling ill. I listen to Harry mourn; I listen as Mother drains him of his grief.

After school I usually walk home through the park. Most of the other kids flock to the corner shop to stock up on sugar or cheap cider and fags. I always hang back in the library for twenty minutes and then slip through the new housing estate. This way I manage to avoid all but the slowest and the dumbest of the other pupils, those who have no real reason to rush home to yet another evening of domestic abuse. The short walk along the tree-lined footpath of the park is the highlight of the day. I usually cut through the landscaped garden and walk through the bandstand, where I stop for a moment and listen to the wind cutting through the trees. If I close my eyes it sounds like music. I hold on to the rail and try and put the whole miserable school day behind me; I let nature carry me away.

I walk along the footpath and take from my pocket the wooden tiger that Joseph carved for me and left in the mill. I look down at it and smile, admiring the smooth slope of its body. As I run my hand along it, I imagine I am running my fingers over the sculpted contours of Joseph's shoulders and the ridges of vertebrae along his back. I feel a rush of heat in the centre of my body; my legs feel shaky and I wonder if I might topple to the ground.

I reach the bandstand, climb the steps, and reach for the handrail that marks out its circumference. I try and regulate my breathing and block out all images of Joseph and his glistening back. My fingers brush the intricate face of the tiger, reading the carved mask like Braille. Each sanded detail is an expression of love.

"I know that smell," a voice behind me says. "It's the retaardvark from the river. Your precious dolly ever float back home?"

The sound of spiteful giggling fills me with dread. I turn around and see the bovine gaze of Penny and Genna, watching me from the other side of the bandstand. I quickly slide the tiger back inside my coat pocket, but my fingers betray me and I see Genna's eyes light up.

"What's that, Elizabeth? A treasure from your sweetheart?"

Penny laughs and I feel my cheeks turn red.

"Shit!" Penny says. "It is! Quick, Gen, I want to see what it is."

Before I can move, the two girls have crossed the wooden boards and hemmed me in against the rail. I can smell peppermint on Genna's perfect breath.

"It's nothing," I say. "Just something my Nan gave me. Like a lucky charm."

Genna holds out her hand. "Show us what it is and we'll leave you alone. Won't we, Pen?"

Penny crosses her heart and smiles. "Absolutely."

I consider trying to break through their feeble cordon, but realise that no matter how far I manage to get, one or the other of them will eventually catch me and make me pay for trying to escape.

I take the tiger from my pocket and reluctantly hold it up to the light. "I have to return it," I say quickly. "My Nan's expecting it back tonight."

Genna snatches it from my hand. I sense a weight shift inside me and feel the urge to knock her off her feet. Genna's oily fingerprints will be all over Joseph's gift; the thought is powerful enough to make me feel sick. She stares at it, unimpressed, and turns it over in her hand.

"Let's see how lucky it is," she says, and hurls it onto the wooden boards of the bandstand.

I watch, horrified, as the tiger flips in mid-air and comes crashing down on the deck, the impact smashing it in half.

"Huh," Genna says, laughing. "Not as lucky as you might think."

I hear myself scream out and then launch myself at Genna, my face contorted in rage, my hands reaching instinctively for her throat. I want to curse and wail at her, but find I'm struggling to take air into my lungs. It doesn't matter; I want my fists and teeth to do my talking for me. I want to rip this bitch's face off and feed it to the dogs.

I lunge again, trying to gain some purchase on Genna's retreating body, but Penny is suddenly between us and the element of surprise is lost. I form a tiny, meaningful fist and swing it wildly and feel it connect with Penny's jaw; I feel a stab of elation and realise that, whatever happens from this moment on, I need to act fast. If they overpower me I'm in deep trouble. I have to keep swinging my fists. I've landed the first blow and I know the consequences will be dire—but God, it feels sweet to have planted my knuckles in Penny's shocked, imperfect face.

She is still reeling from the blow I've dealt her. I lower my head and make a claw with my hand. I rake my nails down her face and feel a sense of primal delirium at the sight of blood. She'll have matching scars, I think. When she next looks in the mirror she'll be reminded of me; I've added to her misery and by Christ it feels good...

My feeling of triumph lasts only as long as it takes to raise my head and see Genna powering in towards me. She floors me with two heavy punches to the face and then both of them set upon me. They are screaming abuse at me, and I curl into a ball with my arms over my head in an attempt to protect my skull. Their own primal rage has possessed them and they are repeatedly kicking and punching me. I open my eyes, and through the gap between my arms and the flailing legs I see the two broken pieces of the tiger. Its face—that carved, beautiful face—is watching me and I feel myself floating away. I distantly wonder why no one has intervened, but my ability to hold on to any thought for longer than a second is disappearing fast.

I've no idea how long the twins beat me, but I know I drift in and out of consciousness for a while. My body is howling in pain, but the dull throbbing feels almost like it belongs to someone else. I turn my cheek on the deck of the bandstand and feel the rough abrasion of the wood. I imagine I can hear music, but it is only the sound of the girls' violence, travelling up through the boughs of the trees. I can smell blood and wonder where it's coming from before I realise that it must be my own. My lips are starting to swell up and my eyes are starting to close; I wonder what new shape my face will assume if I'm lucky enough to make it through the night.

The attack begins to tail off and I risk another glance through swollen eyes at my assailants. All I can see are their black shoes and the white socks covering their lower legs. They are talking to one another, but I only catch every other word. I suspect my ears have been damaged in the attack.

I move my head slightly and peer through the balusters of the bandstand. Positioned no more than thirty feet away is a tall man. He is wearing a black coat. He is watching me with a strange expression on his face. It looks like he is holding a piece of fruit.

I close my eyes, realising that I'm in a worse mess than I could possibly imagine. I look again and the man has disappeared. My mind is correcting itself; he was never there in the first place. He can't have been. It's just my beaten brain reaching out for hope when the cold, logical part knows there is none. It's just me and the twins, and the smashed tiger, marking the point at which all of this began.

I feel the vibration of the twins' movement through the wooden boards and wonder what they're planning next. The beating is clearly over, but the fact that they're still in the bandstand, whispering to one another, suggests that they haven't quite finished with me. There is a final violation that they intend to inflict; a definitive humiliation that they are convinced I will never forget.

I feel hands exerting a rough pressure on my clothes and it suddenly sinks in. I put up as much of a struggle as my bruised body will allow, but it's not even close to being forceful enough. They remove my coat and my blouse and pinch my skin for good measure, calling me the kind of names I've grown accustomed to from the schoolyard. My shoes and socks are kicked off in my vain struggle to retain my dignity and I feel one of the girls pin my shoulders to the ground. The other one sits on my legs and pulls off my skirt and pants.

They both start to laugh. "Look at that," Genna says. "Little Lizzie Rawcunt's as bald as a coot. Not a hair in sight!"

I try to scream and from somewhere I find the energy to thrash my legs. But it's too late; the twins have had their fun and they slowly release me. I can hear them cackling to one another and chanting that horrible name. I lie on the boards of the bandstand, naked and shivering. Despite myself, I start to cry; I hate myself for it, but I can't control it. The tears come anyway, squeezing between the swollen lids of my eyes.

I look up and see Genna and Penny gazing towards the sky. Genna is throwing my clothes onto the roof of the bandstand. She looks across at me and holds up my pants; they are pink with leaping dolphins on the front. She holds them aloft and whoops loudly as though they are the spoils of war, the last item to be thrown, the ultimate symbol of my humiliation and shame.

I catch her eye and she smiles at me; with a grunt, she hurls my underwear on to the roof.

"Have fun getting home, cunt," she says.

I hear them both laugh and then they're gone, their amusement carried back to me on the swirling wind through the trees. I lie there, unmoving. I have no idea what to do next. It feels peaceful down here; like being underwater, cool and reassuring. I close my eyes and go in search of sleep. Just for a second or two, while the water surrounds me and the darkness holds me safely in its hand.

When I come round, grey shadows are descending on the park. The wind is picking up and the trees, no longer catching the sun, are starting to appear more ominous in the fading light. My head is throbbing and my body feels like a war zone, every muscle and sinew kicked raw. I try to raise my head and the bandstand starts to spin; I touch the tender parts of my face, alarmed by the strange shapes my hands encounter.

I glance down and my body goes cold, remembering. I am fully clothed. The underwear, the skirt, the blouse, the coat, the white school socks, even my scuffed black shoes: all have been lovingly replaced.

My eyes dart around the bandstand and beyond, looking for whoever's responsible. There is a chill deep inside my heart.

I glance down at the wooden boards and see the two halves of the tiger, carefully rearranged beside my hand. Next to it is an orange object that looks like an elongated egg. It is a piece of fruit. A simple offering from a stranger that I'm too traumatised and exhausted to understand.

I make my way slowly to my grandparents' house, not yet ready to face Mother with a lie about how I injured myself. I thought it better to try it out on Nan first.

The journey from the park to the house is a difficult one. I run a quick inventory of my body and, though every muscle aches from where the girls have repeatedly kicked me, there is no blood. The real damage—the injuries Nan and Mother will call me to account on—is to my face, which feels like swollen pulp.

I walk carefully over the ridge and past the mill towards the house. I put my hand in my coat pocket and feel the halves of the broken tiger. Just touching the smooth wood leaves me feeling hollow with anger and shame; that I wasn't able to protect it is like a dagger to the heart. I feel around in my other pocket and my fingers brush against the waxy sphere of the fruit. It makes me feel uncomfortable; not the fruit itself, but what it represents: the moment a stranger dressed me as I lay unconscious on the ground.

I finally arrive at the house and knock gently on the door. I hear Nan inviting me in and I turn the handle and cross the threshold. She is in the kitchen baking bread. It smells delicious: fresh and yeasty like warm toast.

She takes one look at me and throws her floury hands into the air.

"Good Lord!" she says. "You look like a creature from a horror movie! What the devil happened, girl?"

She shuffles over to me and starts fussing with my coat, urging me to sit on one of the kitchen stools. I let Nan remove my coat and sit myself down. I want to cry but somehow manage to hold it in. The tears will have to wait till I'm in bed; adult intervention in any of this would be a disaster. I look up at the bright light and blink back the tears, telling myself to be strong. The truth is on the tip of my tongue and I want to tell Nan everything, but to do so would invite all manner of appalling consequences. I have to stick to the story I've already planned.

"I had an accident," I say, feeling stupid. "I fell down a flight of stairs after school. It bashed me up pretty good. Can you help me get cleaned up before I go home?"

Nan looks at me for a long moment; the truth hangs in the silence. Then she nods and begins to tut.

"Those stairs must have fists of iron," she says. "I've met a few flights like that in my time. Horrible, just horrible."

She gives me a cuddle and I feel my resolve start to slip; a single tear falls from my swollen left eye and I wipe it away before Nan sees it.

"Where's Grampa?" I ask.

Nan opens a cupboard and pulls out a green first aid box. "Sleeping off another maggot attack," she says, smiling. I look at her and feel instantly relaxed; somehow I manage to smile back.

She unfastens the first aid box and removes several antiseptic wipes, which she opens. She tenderly begins to clean the blood from my face.

"Didn't you see the school nurse after your fall?"

I hesitate for a second. "I told you. It was after school. I felt such a fool I just wanted to come here. I knew you'd sort me out, Nan. Besides, the school nurse is a grump. She's not very gentle, either."

Nan pauses as she opens another wipe. "Do you see her often?" she says.

I look up and see Nan staring into my eyes; I can see the bright green ring of her iris.

"Sometimes," I say, looking away.

She falls silent and continues to cleanse my face.

"Do you have any other injuries?" she says after a while.

"I'm a little sore, but nothing too bad. It probably looks worse that it is."

"I doubt that," Nan mutters, but she doesn't pursue it and instead starts applying cream to several areas around my eye and cheek. After several minutes' attention, she packs away the first aid box and washes her hands.

"About the best I can do," she says. "My advice: in future stay away from troublesome stairs."

I nod my head and thank her for looking after me. She helps me back into my coat and I give her another cuddle. An idea occurs to me and I take the fruit from my pocket.

"Do you know what this is, Nan?"

She stares at the orange sphere. "Looks like a kumquat," she says. "Where on earth did you get it?"

"A friend gave it to me," I say.

I look at the fruit and remember being naked and bruised on the bandstand. The sight of it provokes a confusing mix of fear and gratitude. I wonder if the kumquat could have been another gift from Joseph, and then the idea that he might have seen me spread out on the boards, unconscious and exposed, fills me with horror and I feel my cheeks going an even deeper shade of red.

I return the fruit to my pocket and move quickly towards the door.

"Love to Grampa," I say.

"Take care of yourself," Nan replies, "and don't worry about your Mother. She might be more understanding than you think. When your father was around, she used to fall down the stairs a lot, too."

As it turns out, Mother is preoccupied with a dilemma of her own by the time I finally return home. I shouldn't really have expected anything less; she is the most self-absorbed person I know. I walk through the front door just as she is scurrying around the house in search of a missing shoe.

"Don't take off your coat," she says, without glancing up. "One of my code red wackadoos is in the middle of a full-blown crisis. I need your support."

A knot begins to form in the pit of my stomach.

"Which one?"

"Funeral Lou, and I don't want any of your snide remarks, either. He happens to be a very sensitive soul." She looks at me as she scuttles past. "What the hell happened to your face?"

I turn away in an attempt to conceal the worst of the bruises darkening my skin.

"I fell down a flight of stairs," I say. "It's nothing."

"Doesn't look like nothing. Looks like you've been hit in the face with a bag of spanners. Who cleaned you up?"

"The school nurse," I say quickly. "She said I'll be back to normal by the end of the week."

"I hope so, Hon, because your face looks like a bashed up peach," she says, reminding me of the orange fruit in my coat pocket. "Maybe we can get Lou to work on you in the parlour, make you look like a real person again."

She laughs and resumes her search for the missing shoe. I feel another unpleasant knot in my gut at the mention of Lou's name and imagine him leaning over me with his cosmetics tray and that troubled smile of his. The idea of him grooming the dead and then turning those same powders and oils on me is repugnant. Even if I was dead I think I'd find a way to object.

Funeral Lou is Mother's only regular. He runs the funeral home on the outskirts of the village, and has been using Mother to alleviate his grief for many years. He grows emotionally attached to the bodies he has been commissioned to prepare for burial, and Mother's job is to respond to any emergency and help talk him through the pain. I suspect she does a little more than that, and Funeral Lou is happy to pay for the service she provides; whenever I've been there his howls of anguish have often turned into moans of pleasure, with only my mother's soothing hand differentiating the two.

She finally locates the shoe beneath the kitchen table and slips it on. Her hand rests on the evening newspaper and she slides it towards me.

"You know her?" she says.

I look at the school photo of a small girl printed on the front page. She is smiling broadly and missing a tooth. The gap looks terribly black. Her face is vaguely familiar but she isn't someone I could put a name to. I shake my head and stare at the sombre headline: **STILL MISSING**.

"You ought to be careful," Mother says. "There could be a pervert in the village. There's plenty of 'em about, you know."

I reach into my coat and touch the fruit; it feels warm and solid. It makes me feel safe. I'm starting to consider it in a completely different light, regarding it as the gift of redemption in a world that offers nothing but missing girls and unloved men. Perhaps one day things will be different; the fruit gives me hope and lets me imagine somewhere brighter, if only for a fractured minute. That somewhere out there is the place where these things grow; a place blessed with exotic fruit that will fall freely into my waiting hand.

I watch Mother slip into her suede jacket before gathering up her bag and steering us out of the house. We climb into our ageing red car, which fails on us more times than it starts, and after a few moments' coaxing from Mother, we're rattling towards Funeral Lou's.

The short drive is silent and uncomfortable. Mother and I have never been good making small talk with each other and today is no different. For once I'm relieved, given that there are countless questions she could have asked about my face. I sit in the passenger seat and feel the muscles in my body starting to seize up; the next few days are going to be rough and I briefly consider whether I might be able to convince Mother that I have the flu so I can stay in bed and allow my body to heal itself in peace.

We arrive at the funeral home and Mother guides the car round the back of the main building, towards the small parlour where Lou does most of his work. Despite their dependence on one another, neither Lou nor Mother are particularly keen for the rest of the community to know of their long-standing arrangement. It wouldn't be good for either business.

She parks the car and looks at me.

"Remember, he gets fifteen minutes and then we're gone. Not a minute more. If he's being needier than usual I want you to come upstairs and rescue me. That face of yours should be enough to halt anyone's grief."

She climbs from the car and then she's gone, moving awkwardly over the cobbles towards the parlour door. She opens her bag, takes out her own key which Lou entrusted her with many years ago, and disappears into the building.

As soon as Mother pushes open the parlour door I can hear the girlish wailing of Funeral Lou.

I sigh heavily and drag myself out of the car. Of all of Mother's appalling 'men friends', I pity Lou the most. The men Mother consoles are a pathetic mess, like creatures turned inside out and captured at their weakest point. They are as horrified by their need for Mother's false love as they are by her unethical willingness to lease it, but at least most of these men are genuinely in torment; at least most of them have suffered crushing grief and heartache that Mother is in a position to help relieve. Lou is a different case altogether. His grief is unnatural, not so much an emotional barrier to be navigated, but an illness; a weird, distasteful condition that Mother knowingly compounds by pandering to his most basic desires. Each time I think of it, and every time I have the misfortune of meeting him, the whole arrangement makes me feel sick. Funeral Lou is a fraud, and everyone involved in this miserable charade knows it.

I enter the parlour and see Mother seated on a long cushioned bench talking slowly to Lou. He looks like he has been weeping for several hours. On the mortuary table I can see a large body. It is Mrs Tavistock, the lady who runs the village shop. Mother told me she had passed away earlier in the week. The shop had closed for two days and we ran out of bread. Mother had called her a *lazy old cow* and had been forced to drive to the supermarket, muttering obscenities under her breath.

"You sit here with this poor dear," she says to me now, feigning sympathy, "and remember to show some respect. Lou and I will be busy for a few minutes, won't we, dear?"

Lou nods eagerly, his eyes looking brighter already. Mother's presence alone seems to have roused his spirits. His hang-dog expression has been transformed into puppy-dog love.

Mother sends Lou scuttling out of the parlour and up the stairs to the 'condolence room'. He can't clamber up there fast enough.

"Remember," she says, "fifteen minutes. You can keep yourself entertained by admiring Lou's latest work of art." She glances at Mrs Tavistock and turns up her nose. "At least the old bird looks better than you. Perhaps you could experiment with some of the make-up while I'm gone. Try and tone down some of the black."

She turns away and ascends the stairs. I sit there feeling cold and shaken. My joints are aching and my head is throbbing. I feel like trading places with Mrs Tavistock. Mother's right: she looks like she has more life left in her than I do. When I touch my face all I can feel are contusions. I vow not to look at myself in the mirror for at least two days. I don't want to see the monster those bitches have turned me into. If I'm subjected to that I'm liable to unravel again, and I'm determined not to allow that to happen. Penny and Genna have reduced me enough; I will fall no further than the unholy place in which I'm currently housed. I swear to it. When you reach the place of the dead, where else is there left to go?

I laugh at my own weak attempt at gallows humour and gather myself for one final push to ease me through the remainder of the day. I rise to my feet and approach the mortuary table, intrigued despite my better judgement as to how Funeral Lou has set about improving the stony appearance of his latest corpse.

I stare at Mrs Tavistock lying motionless on the steel table. She has a modesty cloth placed over her genitals, but the rest of her body is naked. She is slick with disinfectant where Lou has washed her, and her face is heavily powdered. When I lean closer I can just detect a tiny black seam where her mouth has been stitched together. Her eyes are tightly closed and Lou once delighted in telling me that he uses cotton wool to pack out the lid in the same way that the eyeball would have done, before adding plastic eye caps to keep the lids firmly sealed while he works. I'm particularly grateful for this. The idea of seeing Mrs Tavistock glaring at me with those beady, suspicious eyes would have been too much. I think I might have screamed the place down. The parlour reeks of baby powder and hair gel and formaldehyde, and I can feel my stomach starting to turn as the combined odours and the harrowing image of Mrs Tavistock's unnaturally calm features spin me into a lightheaded daze. When I look at the corpse again, I don't see Mrs Tavistock; I see myself, naked and alone on the steel table. My dead body is black and blue. There is nothing Funeral Lou can do with his chemicals and his make-up to disguise the fact that I've been beaten to a grisly pulp.

I turn away, feeling nauseous, my head pounding. As I glance at Mrs Tavistock one last time I see that she has the made-up face of a whore and I think of Mother, working upstairs, counselling Lou in the only way that she knows how.

I hear a noise behind me and look round to see Mother re-entering the parlour, with Funeral Lou trailing sheepishly behind.

"All done," she says, unconsciously wiping her hands on her skirt. "Just needed a little TLC, didn't you, Lou?"

He stares at me and nods, his gravel-coloured eyes and warthog nose repulsing me. I peer closely at him, looking for any sign of lingering grief, but he appears emotionally cleansed. My mother truly does have healing hands.

She offers a curt wave to Lou and ushers me out of the parlour and onto the cobbles. My head hurts worse than ever. We climb back into the car. Mother silently drives us home.

*T*he man stood in the park, beneath the oak tree, waiting for the two girls. He knew what they looked like; their faces were imprinted on his brain. They had come to inhabit the bad thoughts and had drawn him into a troubled sleep for the last two nights. There was nothing he wanted to do more than to show them the fruit; when they saw how pale the flesh was inside, they might start to realise their mistake.

He waited patiently, watching many of the children pass by. They were faceless and of no interest to him. They all looked exactly the same. The two he wanted were different; their blood ran thick with bile, and they concealed a resentment he had witnessed first-hand.

He felt the weight of the dragon fruit in his hand and was reassured by the complexity of its design. It looked beautiful, a bright pink oval with scaly horns protruding from its skin; unlike any other fruit he'd ever seen. It was strange enough to seduce Eve at her most resilient, he thought, smiling.

Another quick glance along the footpath and his patience was finally rewarded. The two girls he wanted were approaching the tree. He sensed their arrogance, even from here, and knew they would stop to talk to him. They thought themselves invincible, like so many others. Walking with a companion always offered a false sense of security; it was the one thing he could be assured of in situations like this: the illusion of safety in numbers.

He allowed the girls to get closer before presenting himself and making sure they received an unimpeded view of the fruit. The girl with the scar on her face looked wary, but the other one, the girl with the flowing golden hair and the butterfly eyes, was intrigued.

"Is that some kind of fruit?" she asked.

The man nodded, holding the dragon fruit to the light. "I just found it. There's a pile of them down the road there, just lying under a tree. I'm taking it home to see what's inside."

He made to walk off and the perfect girl called him back.

"Whereabouts are they?"

The man turned his head and frowned, as if he'd already dismissed them.

"What?"

"The tree. Whereabouts is it?"

The other girl muttered something to her and tried to pull her away, but Little Miss Perfect was not accustomed to being denied anything. She wanted a fruit of her own to take home, just like the man's. They were lying freely available underneath a tree; she just had to find out where.

"It's back there a ways," the man said, waving his hand in the general direction of the park. "But it's pretty difficult to find. It's set right back from the footpath. I only stumbled upon it by mistake. Pretty glad I did, though. Found me a real treasure here."

He smiled and waited.

"What do you think it is?"

The man shrugged. "No idea. But I intend to find out." He offered the girls another perfunctory smile and took half a dozen steps in the opposite direction.

"Could you show us where the tree is?" Little Miss Perfect called, stopping him in his tracks.

He made a show of consulting his watch and looking like it was a major inconvenience, before he turned around and walked back to them.

"Guess I can spare a minute or two," he said, smiling.

Little Miss Perfect grinned. Her sister looked unconvinced. It didn't matter; the pretty girls always got what they wanted. That's the way the world worked. You just had to remind them from time to time what it was that they couldn't live without. Sometimes you had to show them the fruit.

I somehow manage to convince Mother that I'm not well enough to attend school and she allows me to stay home. I lie in bed and take medication for the pain. After about twelve hours I can feel my muscles relaxing, conforming to my new body shape. I can actually feel the swollen tissue contract. After two days of slow recovery I'm ready to face the world again. I stumble into the bathroom and take a look at myself in the mirror. The swelling around my eyes has started to go down, but the bruises have turned an ugly yellow-green colour. I smile and consider how great this would look if it were Hallowecn; my face looks like the belly of a frog. The stiffness in my back and legs has receded and the painkillers Mother keeps dosing me with are keeping most of the discomfort at bay. What I need now is to get the joints working again and remind my body what its job is. An early morning walk would be perfect. I decide to take a stroll over to Langton's farm to see Harry. I realise I can't allow the last horrifying time I saw him, mourning unpleasantly in my Mother's arms, to put me off ever seeing him again. I consider Harry a good friend; I simply don't have enough of them to discard one every time a human frailty is exposed.

I prepare the cold toast and the thermos of black coffee and pull on my heavy coat and boots. When I step outside the sun is rising brightly and trying to burn off the early morning mist. I can hear birds communicating in the trees. In the distance, lorries go thundering by on the main road.

I make my way across Sealer's Ridge and down towards the field where Harry usually works. I see him, hacking away at the stubborn land, and take up my position on the gate. I keep waving until I catch his eye; eventually he sees me and waves back. I watch him as he walks across the dark, unyielding earth.

"Hello, stranger," he says. He notices the colour of my face and his eyes grow wide; his brow becomes as furrowed as the land over which he's just walked. "What in God's name happened to you, child?" he says. "You look terrible."

"This is the PG version," I say, trying to smile. "Mother banned the X-rated version from walking the streets. I've been confined to my bed. That's why I've not been able to bring you your breakfast, Harry. Sorry about that."

Harry waves my apology away as though this is the very last thing on his mind. He is concerned with far graver matters, such as who is responsible for turning me into a punch bag. For the first few minutes, I sit uneasily on the gate, unable to look him fully in the eye. My last sighting of him, looking vulnerable and aroused in my mother's arms, is proving harder to eradicate than I thought, but his concern for my welfare is so genuine, so heartfelt, I chide myself for behaving like an immature kid. I gaze deep into his kind eyes and see reflected there the kind of affection I've always dreamed of seeing in my own father's face as he looks upon me for the first time. I remember Harry saying: *There's something in your blood and theirs that changes everything the minute you're born,* and I find myself wishing for the impossible, that in the volatile world I inhabit, Harry Langton might one day declare himself my dad. It makes me close my eyes for a moment as I try to control the gentle squeezing of my heart. When I open them again, Harry is staring at me, waiting patiently for me to explain how my face came to resemble the belly of a frog. I find myself laughing and crying at the same time, angry at myself for allowing my emotions to run loose, and confused by the chaotic spread of my own pent-up feelings towards my father which, until that point, I hadn't openly considered in years.

"Are you okay?" Harry says, holding on to my left arm, clearly afraid I might topple from the gate.

I nod and wipe away the tears, just relieved that I can look at my friend again without seeing the back of my mother's quivering head.

"I'm fine, Harry. I'm just glad to be out in the fresh air again. When you're cooped up inside, you forget how liberating it is."

"Sometimes," Harry says, "it's easy to lose sight of the tiny miracles that surround us every day. Like all this." He indicates the field and the hills with a wave of his hand.

"You hungry?" I say, holding up the Tupperware and the thermos.

"You kidding? I've a two-day hole to fill."

I smile and hand over the breakfast I've prepared for him. I watch him break into it and take a long slug of the hot black coffee.

"So," he says, between mouthfuls of cold toast. "What's the story?"

I suddenly feel reluctant to relate the details, the memory of my encounter with Penny and Genna having grown darker and more unsettling with each passing day.

"It was just kids at school," I say. "I should have been more careful."

Harry watches me for a moment and says nothing. Then he nods and takes another crunch into the toast.

"What about you?" I say. "How have you been, Harry, stuck out here all on your own? Did you miss me?" I'm aiming for a lightness of tone that might deflect from my own discomfort at being asked about the fight, but I wince at my clumsy choice of words. Harry doesn't need reminding that he's all alone; this is precisely why he's been seeking Mother's unconventional form of counselling. To temporarily cauterise the pain of living night after night in an empty home.

He offers a weak smile and says: "I always miss you, Ellie. But I miss the toast and the hot coffee more."

He cuffs me round the head and this time the smile is brighter, more playful, more sincere.

I jump down from the gate.

"Good," I say, "'cause that's about all I can make."

Harry laughs. "Look after yourself, Ellie, and watch that face of yours. You need lots of ice and vitamin C."

I wave and trudge slowly back the way I came. "See you tomorrow, Harry," I say, glancing over my shoulder; but he's already out of earshot, cutting a lonely figure striding across the black pleats of the earth.

After school I walk home along the ridge and visit the abandoned mill. Both Genna and Penny have been absent from school all day and I'm hoping my good fortune might hold for another few hours, and present me with a replacement for the broken tiger. The two halves of the damaged animal are in my pocket and I reach in and touch them, feeling a fresh stirring of anger and loss. I see myself lying in the bandstand staring at the smashed carving and the incongruous orange eye of the fruit.

I work my way through the basement of the mill and emerge into the shell of the deserted factory. Dull light plays across the littered floor. The retired machines haven't altered since my first visit several years before; they let me pass without making a sound.

When I reach the space at the far end of the mill I glance at the table. I expect to see another carved animal, placed there just for me but this time there is nothing, just a new layer of undisturbed dust. I feel a deep sense of disappointment and turn round to leave, only to see Joseph standing ten feet away from me. He is smiling. He looks different, clean and fully clothed, and it feels like the second disappointment of the day.

"Hello," he says. "You must be the girl who stole my tiger." He is still smiling, but it doesn't look wholly convincing, as though behind it there lies something colder, something unpleasant that I can't quite define.

"I thought you left it here for me," I say, feeling stupid.

The boy stares at me. "Why would I do that?"

I look at him and realise I've made a terrible, ridiculous mistake.

"Didn't you see me?" I say. "I watched you carve it. I thought you knew."

The boy draws his eyes into narrow slits. "Have you been spying on me?" he says.

I shake my head. "Of course not."

"Then how do you know about my secret place?"

I try to laugh, but it sounds hollow. "You've misunderstood. I live next door to you. I sometimes see you from my bedroom window. I've seen you carve those beautiful creatures. I thought *you* must have found *my* secret place."

"How would I do that?" he says. "I've never even seen you before."

I feel another arrow strike me in the heart; he doesn't even know I exist. I'm as invisible to him as I am to everyone else. Our secret friendship is an imaginary one, played out exclusively, like all the others, inside my head.

"Have you been stalking me?" he says.

"God, no. I've been coming here for years. Lots of kids do. You must know that."

The boy's face grows dark. "This is my place," he says. "No one's allowed in but me."

I'm starting to feel afraid; the conversation seems to be running along a very disturbed path and I have no idea how to find my way back.

"I'm sorry. I didn't realise. Perhaps I should just go. We appear to have got off on the wrong foot."

I make to leave but the boy blocks my path. I remember him in the dusk with his dark hair full of sawdust and his powerful upper body glistening with sweat. He is watching me very closely; his eyes look cruel in the dim light.

"No one leaves until I say," he whispers. "I want my tiger back. The one you stole from my secret place."

I briefly wonder how I could ever have felt anything but fear and loathing for this individual, but the thought dissipates fast and I focus instead on the implacable face of the boy I called Joseph, the one I dreamed about in the far reaches of the night.

"I don't have it," I say, feeling the two pieces of the carving clink together in my coat pocket. "I gave it away."

The boy moves to within an inch of my face. His skin is greasy; his eyes have an unforgiving brightness to them that he uses to probe deep inside my soul.

"Then you'd better get it back," he says, "before all the other animals in the zoo turn nasty."

He laughs at that and I feel warm flecks of saliva on my face.

"What if it's broken or lost?"

He leans in even closer, all trace of humour gone from his face.

"But it won't *be* broken or lost, will it?" he says. "Every animal I carve is a good luck charm. Break it or lose it and you kiss goodbye to good luck forever. Don't you know anything?"

I hold my breath, failing to follow the fractured logic of his words. Whatever world he lives in I want no part of it; I just want him to move so that I can run flat out across the field to Nan's. I secretly vow never to enter the mill again. This sinister exchange with the boy has suddenly made me see it for what it really is: a home to the forsaken and the damned. I'll be happy if I never set foot in the place again.

"You can leave the tiger by my back door," he says, smiling and stepping aside. "After all, it's not as if I'd have to travel far to find you, is it, neighbour?"

The threat hangs in the air. I watch him for a moment, dark and unmoving. I flee before he changes his mind.

Two days later and there is still no sign of Penny and Genna. Mother is sitting at the kitchen table, her head buried in the newspaper. I can see the pictures of the girls on the front page. The headline reads: **'Our Precious Angels'**. There is a smaller photo of the twins' parents, weeping at a press conference. They look like they have already started grieving. I wonder where the girls have gone and momentarily consider if I might have been the last person to see them alive. It is a ghoulish thought and I quickly dislodge it, feeling uncomfortable. Penny and Genna aren't dead; even to think such a thing is obscene. Besides, life's never that benign. I have no doubt that I will be forced to spend the rest of my childhood evading the spiteful advances of these two hideous creatures. Add to this my newfound nemesis next door and it's quite the complement of horrors that I seem to have attracted.

I turn my attention away from the paper and resume chopping the mushrooms and onion for tonight's dinner. The noise of the steel knife on the glass chopping board sounds like someone's tapping at the window to be let in. I imagine Joseph clawing at the rotten frame, his face contorted, coming in search of his broken tiger. He is muttering something about good luck turning bad. His eyes are wild and black.

I finish chopping and throw the mushrooms and onion into the frying pan with the sizzling mince. The red meat has turned brown and is cooking in its own fat. The air is thick with steam.

I hear Mother lower the paper and see her peering at me over the top of her reading glasses.

"These girls," she says, "I don't like the look of them. Too perfect. Especially this one."

I feel a warmth in my belly as Mother identifies at a stroke the fault line that runs through the twins' heart. We don't have much in common, Mother and I, but apparently an open mistrust of Penny and Genna is something we both share. Given the circumstances, it seems morbidly inappropriate, but moments of enrichment are rare between us and, when they present themselves, I'm happy to accept them for what they are, no questions asked.

"They'll turn up," I say. "Bad pennies always do." We both realise at the same time that I've made a feeble joke and we laugh together, more loudly than perhaps we should, not so much at the pun, but at how pathetic it is. It is another curious moment and I think Mother senses it too; I don't think either of us can recall the last time we laughed spontaneously and meant it. I'm not even sure we ever have.

I pour two cans of chopped tomatoes into the frying pan and continue to stir. It smells good; the kitchen has that warm, indulgent feel to it that is only really present when food is being prepared. With me cooking and Mother sat reading at the table, it almost feels like we're a normal family for once. I close my eyes and pretend that somewhere in the house there is a man. He is watching the television perhaps, or shaving, or taking a bath while his girls are in the kitchen making tea. I hear him singing and want to reach out to him. He is the missing ingredient; the figure who haunts the house and never shows himself, no matter how hard I will him to appear.

"They don't even look normal," Mother says, drawing my attention back to the photos on the front of the newspaper. "It's too creepy. They look like they've been bred in a laboratory."

I stifle another laugh and stir the lasagne mix into the pan.

"They could be trapped somewhere, Mother. How would you feel then?"

She looks up at the ceiling for a moment, thinking.

"Not altogether displeased," she says, and she looks surprised when I break into fresh gales of laughter. When I finally stop, I feel deeply ashamed that Penny and Genna's disappearance seems to have been the source of such amusement between us. That my mother is unable to empathise with the grief and heartache experienced by the girls' parents is only a distant concern. More compelling is the thrill I feel at listening to my mother pass judgement on the very girls who brought me to my knees and kept me confined to my bed, even if she's unaware of my relationship with them. I wonder if she'd be as savage if she knew that they were responsible for my beating, or would such knowledge simply change the whole dynamic of my mother's response? I keep on stirring the meat of the lasagne and allow the heat and the heady aroma guide me away from such thoughts. It's a complicated area and one I'm not particularly keen to probe. My flawed relationship with Mother is best left alone; if it works at all it's because neither one of us has the nerve to poke around in stuff we don't understand.

Mother has dipped her head back inside the newspaper and I bring the meat to a low simmer.

"Would you miss me, Mother," I say, "if I disappeared like those girls?"

The paper falls; she looks at me over her glasses, frowning.

"What a strange question," she says. "Am I allowed some thinking time?"

She smiles and I turn away, unimpressed with her levity. "I'm serious. It's a simple question. You should be able to answer it without any hesitation."

"If it's that simple, Missy, why don't we turn it around? If you did disappear, would *you* miss *me*? Maybe that's the more revealing question."

I pause, trying to frame an answer that best sums up my feelings towards Mother, before realising I've been caught in a very obvious, and very artless, trap.

"That's not the same," I say. "Of course I'd miss you. If I've been kidnapped I'd probably be in agony in a pit of darkness feeling like the world's about to come to an end."

Mother stares at me. "Then that would make two of us, wouldn't it?" she says, before dropping her head back inside the folds of the newspaper.

I stand for a moment listening to the echo of what she's just said. I feel numb. I want to go to her but I don't feel like I can; we both know it's not something either one of us would be comfortable with. Instead, I silently stir the meat. I listen to the ticking of the kitchen clock. I pray that the two girls I despise are safe, and wonder how close they've come to feeling unloved in their perfect life.

The next day I walk home from school through the park, and see a tall man in a black coat standing under a large oak tree. He is holding in his hand a dark green fruit that looks like a cross between a kiwi and a melon. He is smiling at me, confident that I will eventually approach.

I drift off the footpath and make my way towards him. I stop about ten feet away. He nods and cradles the fruit. He is middle-aged and has large puppy-dog eyes. His nose is too big for his face and his lips are a little too wide. He looks like most of the teachers at my school: tired, unremarkable and running to fat. His best years are obviously behind him; all he has left to look forward to are moments like this, when, for a brief time, he wields something of interest again.

"I think I know you, don't I?" I say. "I remember the black coat, and the fruit, of course."

We both smile.

"I wasn't sure you'd recognise me," he says. "Those girls gave you quite a beating. You were pretty much unconscious the whole time."

I remember lying in the bandstand and blush at the thought of this strange man staring down at my naked body. I also remember him retrieving my clothes and dressing me, and realise that the time for false modesty has passed. He has already seen more of me than any other person alive. I briefly consider the missing girls and then realise I am being foolish. If he was going to hurt me he would surely have done so when he had the chance. I have no reason to be afraid, not of this man. He has earned my trust simply by showing me kindness when others might have walked on by. I owe him a debt of gratitude for saving me, for pulling me from the wreckage of the fight. He looks nervous, as though he's remembering too; I smile warmly at him to let him know how pleased I am to see him. He looks mildly confused. He blinks rapidly. He moves the fruit from hand to hand like he's juggling a heavy ball.

"I want to thank you," I say, "for your help a few days ago. I don't know what I'd have done if you hadn't come along."

He nods. "I like the park," he says. "I sometimes watch the world go by from the bandstand. Other times I just wait here. This is my favourite tree."

He stares up into its green canopy and I watch his eyes slowly close; he looks at peace, more so than moments before, and I wonder what he sees in the green leaves and the wide boughs that have the power to transport him away.

"What's your name?" I say.

He pauses and frowns, then softly mutters, "Gregory," as though he were whispering a secret.

"I'm Elizabeth, but my friends call me Ellie." He seems surprised that I am clearly inviting him to do the same.

"It's very nice to meet you, Ellie." He says nothing for a moment; just stands there staring at me, looking closely at the faded bruises around my eyes.

"I'm glad your face is healing," he says. "When I left you I thought it might take weeks before you recovered. You looked terrible."

"I'm stronger than I look. Besides, most people don't look long enough to notice the difference."

He looks puzzled. "Why not?"

I shrug my shoulders and move five feet closer. "I guess I just don't have a very noticeable face," I say.

He seems on the verge of contradicting me, but then changes his mind. He turns and peers towards the bandstand instead.

"How did you get them down?" I ask. "My clothes, after they'd thrown them on the roof."

"I climbed up and got them for you," he says. "I wanted to get the girls that did it right there and then, but I knew you were more important." He blushes slightly and averts his gaze. "When I dressed you I tried to close my eyes the whole time. I didn't want you to wake up and be embarrassed."

I feel a little embarrassed now, so I quickly move the conversation on to something else.

"I like your fruit," I say. "I don't think I've ever seen anything like it before. What is it?"

Gregory looks down as though he's momentarily forgotten what he's holding in his hands.

"It's called a jackfruit," he says. "It's the largest tree-borne fruit in the world. Beautiful, isn't it?"

I nod my head. "It's almost as big as a baby," I say. "Is it heavy?"

Gregory smiles and offers me the fruit. "Here. See for yourself."

I lean forward and take the jackfruit in both my hands. The weight of it takes me by surprise.

"Bloody hell! It's like a sack of spuds from Harry's farm. How does something this size grow on a tree?"

Gregory's smile widens to a grin. "Not all fruit is the same. You just need the imagination to try something different."

I hand it back to him. "Where did you get it?" I ask.

He pauses and looks down at the ground. He seems nervous, unsure of himself; he is blinking uncommonly fast.

"I . . . I found it," he says softly.

"You mean you stole it," I say, realising now why he is looking so agitated.

"No," Gregory says, looking increasingly flustered. "I found it. Stored inside the opening of a badger's sett. There are three of them." He pauses again, clearly reluctant to declare too much information to a stranger, before adding: "I suppose I can even show you if you want."

"How far is it?"

He points down the footpath. "It's a few hundred yards. You might get your clothes dirty, though. You have to duck under some pretty thick gorse in order to see it."

"I don't mind about that," I say, refusing to be dissuaded, despite Gregory's best efforts. "My face can't look any worse, can it?"

I smile and he makes a lame effort to do the same; his face looks sickly, though, as if the thought of returning to the badger's sett has unsettled him. Perhaps the discovery of the jackfruit was fraught with more difficulties than he's letting on; maybe he's trying to protect me from something else, trapped deep inside the gorse, something he thinks I'm too delicate to stomach, like the half-eaten body of a squirrel or the rotting entrails of a fox.

"Don't worry," I say. "I'm much tougher than I look. You don't have anything to worry about, I promise."

"Maybe I should just give you this one," he says, holding out the jackfruit. "That way you won't get into trouble when you get home."

"That wouldn't be fair. This one's yours. If there are two more under the gorse like you said, I can just find my own. With a bit of luck we might even see a badger."

I remember the poor creature I saw on the railway embankment with its stomach gouged out and feel a chill pass down my spine; I wonder how much of the dead animal remains.

"I doubt we'll see a badger," Gregory says. "They mostly come out at night."

"Do they like fruit?"

Gregory frowns. "I suppose so."

I start to feel excited. "Imagine how surprised our badger will be tonight when he leaves his sett. There'll be a feast waiting right outside his door!"

Gregory smiles at my exuberance and his eyes grow suddenly bright.

"Maybe that's what we should do," he says. "Come back here tonight and watch the badgers eat the fruit. We could bring some snacks and have a midnight feast."

I scratch the back of my head and feel as though the ground has abruptly shifted. Gregory's suggestion seems almost improper, and my eagerness of moments before fades away to be replaced by a crashing wave of doubt.

"I don't know," I say. "I don't think I'd be allowed out. Too many kids have gone missing. There's even a curfew."

"But you'll be safe with me," Gregory says. "I'll protect you like I did before, with the girls."

I nod my head but have a different perspective on the matter. Gregory didn't protect me; he only watched from the side as I took a beating and then recovered my clothes and dressed me while I was out cold. I choose not to mention any of this, though I find myself unconsciously retreating, taking several steps back towards the path.

"It's too dangerous," I say. "My mother would blow a gasket. She's a mean old bird, too. Has a devil of a temper."

Far from being discouraged by my reluctance, Gregory seems almost relieved. His enthusiasm for the midnight adventure continues to grow.

"Think about it, Ellie. We can sit and watch the badgers. It has to be better than foraging around in the dirt for fruit."

"I don't think so," I say. "Maybe another time, when the curfew's lifted."

Gregory stares at me and I can see beads of sweat dripping from his temple and gliding down the side of his face. He appears tense; his jaw is set and his eyes are unwavering. I sense that he has arrived at a decision, though what this might be I have no idea.

"If you change your mind," he says, "I'll be waiting here by the tree at midnight. Perhaps, if you decide to come, we'll discover something special together. I might even give you something to remember me by."

He holds the jackfruit aloft and smiles at me. He seems calmer, as though my decision to withdraw from the badger hunt has pleased him. He turns to go and then stops, glancing over his shoulder.

"One last thing," he says. "Those girls, the ones who have disappeared, will you miss them?"

I grope around for a moment for the most sensitive answer and then decide to opt for the truth.

"No," I say. "They made my life miserable. I'm glad they've gone."

Gregory closes his eyes and inhales the cool evening air. "Good," he says, smiling.

He turns and walks off down the footpath, cradling the jackfruit in his hands.

When I arrive home, Mother is in the kitchen waiting for me. She waves the newspaper in front of my face and places it on the table.

"They've been found," she says. "All three girls, floating face down in the river."

I'm a little stunned; I can't summon anything appropriate to say. I stare blankly at the paper, the text and the images blurring.

"How did they die?"

Mother pours herself a glass of water from the tap and looks at me. "Read the damn report like everyone else," she says.

She walks out of the kitchen and slams the door. I stare at the wall and listen to the hollow ticking of the clock.

I spend the rest of the night in my room, watching the furniture grow increasingly dark. I am thinking about Penny and Genna and trying hard not to imagine what they had to endure right at the end. I'm thinking about dead badgers, and strange fruit, and men who silently dress naked girls. I think about Mother and the grief she releases in the endless moans that echo through the house. I am thinking about Joseph and the beautiful animals he carves, watching the terrifying flex of his personality as he prowls around the abandoned mill.

I climb from the bed, as much to stop the barrage of thoughts as anything else, and move to where my coat is draped over the linen basket. I reach into the pocket and pull out the two halves of the carved tiger. Once again I'm compelled to stroke the smooth curve of its broken back. I feel close to weeping, but I can't for the life of me figure out why. It feels like it could be nothing and so many things all at the same time.

I walk to the window and look out at the dark yard next door. There is no sign of the boy. A weak night light shines above the back door; I can see dust and woodchips on the illuminated ground where the boy has carried out his work. I think back to our conversation in the heart of the mill and wonder how his character can be so inconsistent with the beauty of the animals he carves.

You'd better get it back before all the other animals in the zoo turn nasty.

I smile, but it vanishes fast. The line sounds like something out of a cheap gangster film, but at night, with the boy's house in darkness, I confess to being vulnerable to all manner of terrors, no matter how absurd they may initially appear. I wonder how many other creatures he has trapped in there with him, how many carved horrors there are waiting to be unleashed...

I shiver and place the two halves of the tiger on the duvet of the bed. I should just return it, I think. Face up to my fears, step across the yard, and lay the broken pieces outside the door. Another thought occurs to me and I smile to myself. If the boy comes after me for damaging the damn thing, I now have my own enforcer; Gregory, the man with the unusual fruit. I picture his conflicted face as we spoke beneath the oak tree; those blinking eyes, the unruly mop of thinning hair. What was it he had said? *I'll protect you like I did before, with the girls.* I breathe heavily and stare at the tiger. That protection might come in handy after all. I don't like the look of the boy next door; he has the eyes of an habitual bully. It would be a relief to have someone to rely on for once in a fight.

I cast my mind back to that moment again when I first glimpsed Gregory watching me through the balusters of the bandstand. Had I been able to rely on him then? Why had he watched the fight unfold without interceding? Why had he chosen to do nothing until the girls had gone?

These are all questions to which I have no answers, and I push them aside to join all the other unanswered questions I have asked myself over the years. The memory of Gregory stays with me, though. I picture his simple face leaning exquisitely close to mine. *Perhaps, if you decide to come, we'll discover something special together,* he had said. In my mind's eye his face is layered, like an onion, and I'm unable to read all the secrets of his life I imagine each coating of his skin contains. Instead, I just see the man. The one who wanted to show me badgers eating fruit at midnight; who swore he'd protect me from whatever monsters lurked in the shadows; who dressed me with his eyes closed so neither one of us would feel ashamed.

I pick up the two pieces of the tiger, return them to my pocket, and pull on my shoes and coat. I glance at my watch. It is 11:08pm. I listen quietly at my door; Mother is already asleep. I creep down the stairs and pass through the dark kitchen towards the back of the house. Before I leave I grab a piece of fruit from the bowl. Nothing spectacular, just an apple; a fitting gift to Gregory from a friend.

When I step outside I realise just how cold it is and I button my coat; I bury my hands in the pockets and I press the halves of the tiger into my skin. I want it to hurt. I want the carving to dig deep into my flesh so that I'm reminded of how wrong I was about the boy; how dangerous it can be sometimes to idealise a person based solely on what you want them to be.

I walk to the end of the path and glance through the mesh fencing to the yard next door. The boy's house is silent. The night light above the back door seduces a handful of hardy moths. A nocturnal bird passes overhead and I look up at the sky. The enormity of it alarms me; there is hardly any definition to it and I try and lock onto something before I lose myself in the black emptiness. I find myself feeling afraid. I remember lying unconscious on the bandstand. The memory of what came after only feels a heartbeat away, but to retrieve it fully I will have to enter the dark.

I lower my eyes, anxious that if I look up at the sky for too long I might be discouraged from what I'm about to do. It would be so easy to just fall into that vast expanse of darkness and forget everything; to drift away, like smoke, unable to reach out to anyone. To just fall back into the empty arms of space and never wake up; my bruised face nothing more than another dying yellow star in the night sky.

I wonder where the boy is sleeping and peer up at the house. It all looks so calm, so quiet. I climb over the mesh fence and walk up to the back door. I stand beneath the moth-infested light. I pull the broken tiger from my pocket and remember the boy saying, *Break it or lose it and you kiss goodbye to good luck forever. Don't you know anything?* The memory makes me feel cold and confused. Perhaps I don't know anything; nothing important, anyway. Not a single, solitary thing.

I bend down and place the carved tiger on the mat just outside the door. I am returning what I claimed by mistake. Not just the carving, but the friendship I had created in my head. I stare at the tiger and feel a tear at the corner of my eye. It looks diminished, horribly reduced; a symbol of good luck gone bad.

He sat at the kitchen table, a smile playing at the corners of his mouth, remembering his meeting with the girl. Her name was Ellie. He thought she had been kind. She had the face of a disgraced boxer but the pale eyes of an angel. He remembered her smiling a lot.

He closed his eyes. He was pleased that she had liked the fruit. He had picked it out especially for her. The biggest and the best. He wanted her to know she was special; he wanted her to sense it, and she had. He thought that was why she had treated him like a friend.

When the bad thoughts had grown worse, as he knew they would, he didn't think he'd be able to fight it. He'd felt dismayed. The desire to take her away had been so strong. But he had fought it. He had turned the bad thoughts into something else; he had confused everyone, even the girl.

And now, here he was, thinking about the tree, and about Ellie. And about the girls who had been seduced by the fruit.

He smiled again and spent ten minutes collecting together the things he would need. He loaded up the car in darkness. The world was silent. He stood listening for a moment and then realised he was listening to his own bad thoughts, nameless and terrible, echoing deep inside the stillness of his head. He had heard them before, many times, and he let them come; he no longer had the strength to push them away.

I cling to the shadows and make a point of avoiding the sodium wash of the streetlights as I walk quickly towards the park. I wonder whether Gregory will already be there, waiting patiently beneath the oak tree, but decide that if he isn't, I'll watch his arrival from the bandstand. I want my appearance to be a surprise. I want to see his face light up like it did earlier, those wide, rubbery lips parting like a clown's, his sad smile accepting me, taking me in.

As I cross the street I see a fox up ahead. It has stopped in the middle of the road and is watching me intently, without fear. Its eyes blaze yellow; one of its front paws is frozen in mid-air. It is trying to decide what to do. After a moment, it assumes I pose no threat to it and moves on, its tail almost brushing the ground.

When it's gone I realise I have been holding my breath. I wonder if the fox's instinct to fight or flee has been compromised by years of these kind of random encounters. It seems such an inevitable process: fox and human meet in the dark, nothing much happens, and they go their separate ways. It's as if life has been designed to repeat this pattern *ad infinitum,* until eventually one or the other wonders what might happen if the pattern were changed; if the ritual of the dance gains a variable that instantly makes it less easy to define.

These thoughts consume me as I walk and I feel a sense of liberation at the thought of being out this late alone. Everyone knows about the curfew and the three missing girls, but if I was murdered on the street tonight would anybody outside of my immediate family really miss me? Would anyone be moved to tears by the fact that I was gone? A part of me thinks it might be quite romantic to just be removed from the world in which I live overnight; here one minute, gone the next. No heartache, no tears, no mess. I think of all the killers who dream of murdering young girls, and all the young girls whose lives are so miserable they dream endlessly of death. How often do those two worlds collide?

I smile at the arbitrary nature of my thoughts, no doubt triggered by the enveloping darkness, and finally reach the entrance to the park. As the streetlights dwindle I curse myself for failing to bring a torch and spend a few moments adjusting to the deeper dark. The playground in the distance looks sinister and I try to remember what the dark shapes represent. I've played on them all countless times, but I've never seen them quite like this. The difference leaves me feeling unsettled, a little queasy, as though the world I know so intimately has revealed a side of itself that I never even knew was there. Even the trees and the shrubbery have changed; everything wears a new face, secret surgery conducted in the dark.

I stand beneath the stone arch that marks the entrance to the park and stare in the direction of the large oak tree. Gregory is already there, just as I knew he would be. I cross the freezing grass, listening to it crunch beneath my feet. My heart starts to pump hard inside my chest. I reach inside my pocket and try to focus on a single thought. It doesn't work. I feel the apple and clutch it tightly, trying to squeeze all the darkness away. Gregory is watching me; he was always watching me. I suspect he always will be, too.

I remember him saying: *Other times I just wait here. This is my favourite tree,* and I thank the Lord that he at least has that, no matter what else happens. He has hanged himself from the darkest bough of his beloved oak tree. In death they are forever conjoined.

He swings gently in the night air and I feel suddenly deflated. The stepladder he used has been knocked to the ground. It looks like the tip of an arrow. It is pointing to what Gregory has done. I'm immensely grateful that there is no light and no torch; just this long, swinging shadow of a faceless man, and the appalling smell of a body that has voided itself as it dropped; the last reckoning of a soul that has come to an end.

I look down and see the outline of Gregory's final offering to those he's left behind: a glass bowl filled to the brim with strange fruit. I feel nothing; just emptiness. I sense the weight of the body hanging above me and want to scream, but I don't. Instead, I remove the apple from my pocket and place it gently on top of the bowl. It sits there, my dark contribution; my world and Gregory's, colliding.

Acknowledgements

I OWE A DEBT OF GRATITUDE TO THE FOLLOWING FINE people:

Andrew Jury: long-term friend, trusted critic and most agreeable drinking companion.

Stephen Arnold: loyal friend and connoisseur of first-rate whisky.

The PS Publishing gang, especially Pete & Nicky Crowther, Nick Gevers and Mike Smith: if only all publishers were as charming and professional as you guys.

And, of course, my family, Ethan and Suzanna Cooper, without whose love and support none of my peculiar little tales would ever be told...

JAMES COOPER is the author of the short story collections *You Are The Fly* and *The Beautiful Red*. His novella *Terra Damnata* was published by PS Publishing in 2011 and was shortlisted for a British Fantasy Award. Forthcoming is *Country Dark*, which will be published next year as part of the TTA Novella Series, the novel *Dark Father* from DarkFuse in June 2014, and the short story collection *Human Pieces* from PS Publishing. You can visit his website at: jamescooperfiction.co.uk